INSURMOUNTABLE

Against insurmountable odds one girl's faith finds hope.

ANNA COLAR

A Note from the Author

Insurmountable means "too great to overcome," but through Christ we can do all things. Some people are rejected in families because of family image. If to them you're not smart enough, or you don't acquire a nice home or vehicle, you mostly likely will be the outcast in your family or environment.

Children are rejected at school for more reasons than one. Rejection and its prejudice are everywhere. The word of God says, "The first shall be last and the last shall be first." Be careful if you're first all the time and you reject someone who is least to you. In God's eyes, you are putting yourself in the back and the one you're looking down on in the front. Sometimes the one you discourage is the one you later need help from to encourage you.

As you read this book discover which character(s) you relate to. Too many people see the problem and talk about it instead of helping. The elders are supposed to help the younger generation but some of them can't, as they too are still growing up. How can someone learn or become great if no one has exposed them to it? This is only done through Christ Jesus. He is the only One Who can make the impossible, possible. Therefore, nothing is insurmountable for you in Christ Jesus.

Special Thanks

To Jesus

Thank You, Friend, for having a plan to do me good and not evil. Man may have a plan to reject me but You have a plan that will keep me accepted by You. You have me in your hand and no devil in Hell can pluck me out! You are THE GREAT I AM!

My Parents

I thank God for my mother, Earline A. Guy, for having Bible Study with my sister and me every Saturday morning. Teaching us to fear, love and put God first. She would always tell us to remember, "If you can't make peace don't make war." To my dad, Bruce A. Guy, for being my friend. May you Guy's rest in peace.

Spiritual Parents

Thank you for watering what my mom planted in me. You all poured into me what I believe God anointed you to do in more ways than one. We know that all the increase came from God.

My Husband

Rev. Felton Colar, Jr., you are my everyday dream and my dreams keep coming true. Thank you for investing your belief, moments, prophesy and your life with me during this journey. I believe that God lend you His eye to see what he sees in me.....Greatness! You are patient, kind and gentle with me. Your sweetness never gives me a cavity.

Chapter One

Mariah was rudely awakened from an exhilarating dream by the piercing sound of her alarm clock. She so wanted to escape reality and go back to her exciting, perfect life in her dream, but instead she jumps out of bed and begins to get ready for school. This was the first day of school since the Christmas break. Within seconds her mother, Genevieve, bursts through the door, knocking as she enters.

"Mariah, get up! It is 5:45," she shouts. "It is…"

"I'm already up," Mariah interrupted.

Genevieve just smiles to herself and walks out the door. She walks to the next room and knocks on the door. It is her niece's room. After a couple knocks with no response, she slowly opens the door.

"Jasmine, honey, are you up? It is 5:55 now, and you need to get ready for school. The bus will be here soon." There is no response from Jasmine who is still lying in bed.

"Jasmine, hon..."

"Oh, man! I'll get up in ten minutes!" Jasmine shouts angrily from underneath the covers.

"All right, dear. I just don't want you to miss the bus," Genevieve answers sweetly and walks out the door.

Fifteen minutes later, Jasmine enters the bathroom where Mariah is now brushing her teeth. She pushes Mariah out of her way and into the wall. Mariah gives her a puzzled look without pushing back.

"Why did you do that?" she asks with her toothbrush still in her mouth.

"You were in my way!" Jasmine shouts in Mariah's face. Her breath smelled of past meals. Mariah wrinkled her nose from the putrid smell. She finished brushing her teeth and walked away shaking her head.

Mariah goes to her room to finish getting ready for school. After making her bed and tidying up her room, she gathers up her books and goes to the kitchen to have breakfast. She says good morning to her mother as she gets her bowl and pours herself some cereal. Genevieve is cleaning the kitchen. After finishing her cereal she goes to the sink and rinses it out. She places it in the strainer to dry.

"Mariah, dry that out and put it away, please," her mother says without looking up from what she is doing. Mariah reaches for the towel and begins to dry the bowl.

Jasmine walks in with a scowl on her face and grabs a bowl and a box of cereal. She walks over to the table and sits down. As she begins to pour herself some cereal her aunt turns to look at her.

"Well, good morning to you, too, Jasmine!" Genevieve says with a smirk.

"Oh, sorry, Auntie! Good morning."

"You better hurry and eat as much as you can. The bus will be here soon."

As Mariah puts her bowl away, Jasmine stops and looks confused. She glances at the clock over the kitchen sink, which reads 6:38 and then asks her aunt, "Why? What time does the bus come?"

"Between 6:45 and 6:50. Jasmine, you better watch how you respond to me. Remember, I am not your equal."

Jasmine glowers and puts the milk and bowl away. As she walks out of the kitchen she indignantly says, "Whatever!"

"What's with her?" Mariah asks as she walks past her mom.

"That's what happens when you don't wake up on time," Genevieve replied. "You give your emotions the permission to control your day. Be careful with her, Mariah. She's emotional."

"Well, I am not sure what you mean exactly."

"When someone is emotional, anything can be, and usually is, taken the wrong way. Then feelings get hurt. Now, hurry before you miss the bus!"

"Oh, okay. Bye, Momma!" Mariah says as she grabs her things and runs out the door.

"Remember what I said," Genevieve hollers as her daughter runs out of the kitchen.

The bus pulls up to the school. All the kids are watching to see who's wearing what and who has on new clothes. Mariah is in the 8th grade so this is her last year at middle school. Mariah is content with her new clothes. As she steps off the bus she hears a familiar voice.

"Man, this girl still don't have name brand clothes!" Rodney says out loud to those standing around. Several of them laugh.

"If you care so much then buy some," Mariah says as she passes them. "Look at you looking like the Black Knight!"

"Oh, man, that was a good one! She got you, Cuz," Anthony says teasingly. Some of the boys laugh.

"Shut up, Man!" Rodney snaps back angrily. "Look at you, a three ton moose! Look down at my feet. What's my shoe say?" Rodney asks braggingly with a smirk on his face.

"It says you can afford some nice shoes, but what about the clothes?" Anthony retorts.

Just then the school bell rings.

"Man, I don't have time for this!" Rodney says indignantly and heads to his homeroom.

As the bell rings, the students in Ms. Wilkerson's Homeroom class are quickly seated. Mariah glances around the room to see who all is in her homeroom. The teacher, sitting at her desk, looks up from her notes.

"We will begin class with positive affirmations so we can have a new beginning," Ms. Wilkerson says as she gets up and begins to write on the blackboard. "I feel good," she says as she writes out the affirmation on the board, "because I know I will pass this class."

Everyone repeats it except Rodney, who changes the words and sarcastically says, "I feel good because I know Mariah will fail this class." Some of his classmates begin to laugh.

"Well, I don't believe that!" Mariah replies immediately.

"Rodney, would you like to repeat that?" Ms. Wilkerson asks as she turns around and faces him.

"What?" Rodney asks sheepishly.

"I asked if you would like to repeat what you just said and let us all hear what name you used."

Some of the students turned to look at him and giggled.

"Oh, sure!" he said enjoying the attention. "I said, 'I feel good because I know Mariah is going to fail this class."

"Be careful what seeds you plant. Harvest time always pays the sower back in full, whether the crop is good or bad!"

"Harvest time?" Rodney asked bewildered.

Chapter Two

Mrs. Geo, the school counselor, walks to the door of her office with her arms full of papers and books. She is struggling to keep them from falling as she fumbles for her keys to the office. The principal, Mr. Chance, stops for a moment to chat with her on his way to the restroom.

"Well, good morning, Counselor," he says with a pleasant smile on his face.

"Good morning, Mr. Chance," Mrs. Geo replies, still struggling to keep her load from falling to the floor.

"So how was your Christmas break?" the principal asks, noticing her struggle but never offering her assistance.

"Oh, good and not so good, but my good far outweighed the bad," she replied.

"Have things changed yet?" he asks beginning to pry into her business, but still not offering to help ease her load. He has no intention of helping her.

Mrs. Geo is extremely frustrated by now with Mr. Chance. She snaps a quick answer back at him as she sticks the keys in the door, trying hard to keep things balanced. "If not, I will keep speaking change until it does!"

"That's the right attitude!" he says patting her shoulder as he walks away down the hall to the restroom.

Just then the door to her office opens in one quick jerk. As Mrs. Geo steps through the threshold, her arm full of books fall to the floor, and papers scatter everywhere.

"Oh, sure, now you wait to fall! I should have dropped you in front of Mr. Chance just to see if he would have bothered to help."

Mr. Chance sees several boys hanging outside the boys' bathroom. "Gentlemen, you better be getting back to class!" he says as he walks inside the bathroom doors. There is an adolescent boy standing at the sink washing his hands. Mr. Chance is suddenly hit with the urge to go.

"Young man, you are taking entirely too long to wash your hands. Speed it up!"

The young boy gets nervous and grabs some paper towels, hardly taking the time to dry his hands. He quickly wads up the paper and tosses it at the trashcan. He misses, however, in his haste and hits the principal. He quickly runs out the door, but his back gets caught on the handle. It jerks him back. Mr. Chance has now lost patience with the boy and pushes him and his backpack out the door.

He enters a stall and prances back and forth before placing toilet paper on the toilet seat. He sits down and whispers, "Oh, Jesus, help me! Forgive me, Lord, I should've helped Mrs. Geo when I had the chance."

Mr. Chance reflects on the day his great aunt cursed him for not helping her when she was struggling with the laundry.

When Omar Chance was a teenager, his aunt with one fake leg would keep him while his mom was at work. Omar would sit on the sofa and watch his aunt struggle with the laundry basket.

One day as he was playing his video game she walked in front of him with the laundry basket full of clothes to wash, she fell and hurt her ankle. He continue to play the game. Instead of helping her up, he asked if she was okay.

With tears in her eyes, she streched forth her hands and cursed him. "Every time you fail to help a struggling woman close by, the result will come out your rectum like a woman in travail."

Mrs. Geo has finally settled back into her office and just sat down to look over her schedule for the week. Suddenly, there is a faint knock on her door. Without looking up from her computer she hollers, "Come in!"

The door slowly opens and Rodney walks in.

"Rodney, what are you doing here?" Mrs. Geo asks. "It's your first day back from Christmas vacation."

"My teacher told me to come here?" Rodney replies lowering his head.

"What is the problem?" she asks.

"I really don't want to talk about it," he answers without lifting his head.

"Well, you might as well. When you hold things in they manage to find their way out."

"What do you know, Oh Wise One?" Rodney asks sarcastically.

Mrs. Geo removes her reading glasses and sits back in her chair. Looking intently at Rodney she says, "I'm here to help you, Rodney, but I can't help you if you choose to be a mystery. Think about it."

"I can't. I just can't," Rodney says looking up at the counselor.

"All right. I'm here if you need me. In the meantime, go back to class and try not to continue doing what got you sent here today."

Rodney gets up and walks out the door as the principal walks in.

"Mrs. Geo, I need to apologize to you. I'm sorry I did not stop and help you earlier. I had something I needed to take care of right away," Mr. Chance says as he walks in the door.

The bell rings just as Mrs. Geo starts to speak. Pausing for a moment until the noise stops, Mrs. Geo replies, "I'm not worried about that, Mr. Chance."

"Well, I just wanted to apologize in case I offended you," he says smiling as he walks out the door. "Have a good day, counselor."

"You too, sir."

Students are talking with one another in the Home Economics class as they wait for their teacher, Miss Louivere, to arrive. Mariah is sitting in her seat talking with her friend, Janice, who has her eye on Christopher.

"Good morning, class!" Miss Louivere says as she enters the room. "Welcome back to Home Ec. The school year is more than halfway over now, so we need to get to work."

"Miss Lou, what are you going to be teaching us for the rest of the year?" Candace asks, raising her hand.

"I'm going to be teaching you how to cook," she says with a grin.

"It better not be no slop," Damon says trying to be cute. "I can't stand no pigs in a blanket slop."

"You have a problem with me, young man?" Miss Louivere asks with a stern look on her face.

Damon doesn't answer. He just stares at her.

"No? Well, next time you have something to say, raise your hand," she says walking closer to the student. "You do not want to mess with me, Damon. Don't you know I have the power to fail you?" She turns to walk back to the front of the class.

"Whatever!" Damon says with an attitude. "A black man can't speak his mind?"

"Color has NOTHING to do with it," Miss Lou snaps back. Turning around to face Damon again she adds, "Zora Neale Hurston says, 'Speak so you can speak again.' Try reading her book sometime."

Mariah's and Christopher's eyes meet before they smile at each other. Returning to the front of the class, Miss Lou says, "Ok, class, find a lab partner, someone you don't know!"

Christopher makes his way to Mariah smiling, and suddenly Mariah feels uneasy. *Oh, my Gosh! He's coming over to sit here.*

Christopher notices that Mariah is uncomfortable.

"What? You don't want me to sit here?" he asks.

"It's not that," she replies. "I just thought you would sit with someone else."

"You want me to move?"

"It doesn't matter," she says lowering her head shyly.

"Class, this is where you will sit for the remainder of the year," Mrs. Lou adds.

Janice is filled with jealousy as she sees Chris sitting with Mariah. Janice ends up with a chubby white boy. Damon notices the look on Janice's face and realizes why. He decides to act on it.

Walking over to Christopher he asks, "Dog, what do you think you're doing?"

"Sitting here. What's it look like I'm doing?" Christopher replies sarcastically.

Damon bends down and whispers in Christopher's ear, "Man, Janice is hot! Why you sitting with No Brand?"

"Who is No Brand?" he asks looking confused. Janice hears the conversation and puts her head down on the table.

In the meantime, Miss Lou is going around placing names on the tables. Damon notices what she is doing and says, "Man, Miss Lou, this is kindergarten stuff! Why you going around writing our names on the tables to make sure we don't switch seats?"

Pushing her glasses down to the end of her nose and looking over top of them, she says, "Welcome to Kindergarten!" Everyone laughs.

Damon stomps over to where Janice is sitting, but the chubby guy is sitting there. "Hey, Big Butt, move! I'm sitting here. You go sit in my spot."

The boy is frustrated but goes over to sit by Candace. Janice glances over to see what's going on with Christopher and Mariah.

"So, you must like Christopher, huh?" Damon asks her.

"What?" Janice acts surprised.

"Oh, come on. I see how you look at him," he retorts.

"No, it's not that. I'm just making sure he's not distracting my girl."

"Class, may I have your attention please?" Miss Lou hollers. "On Wednesday we will be making scrambled eggs. You will need to bring your own eggs."

"How many eggs are we to bring, Miss Lou?" Candace asks.

"No more than four per person." The bell rings. "Class dismissed."

Mariah and Christopher are talking on the way out of class. At the end of the day, Christopher catches up with Mariah as she is heading for the bus.

"So, Mariah, can I call you?" he asks walking beside her.

"For what?" she replies looking a little puzzled.

"Just to talk," he says.

"We can do that at school," she hollers back as she runs for the bus. Christopher just stands there watching her and shakes his head.

"Hey, Girl, wait for me!" Janice hollers as she runs to catch up with Mariah. "So, what did he want?"

"My number."

"Did you give it to him?" Janice asks.

"Of course."

"Mariah!"

"Not!" Mariah says laughing.

"Smart! It's obvious he just wants one thing," Janice whispers to Mariah.

"And that is all he is going to get!" Mariah snaps back.

"Wait, what are YOU talking about?" Janice asks a little shocked at Mariah.

"A lab partner!" Mariah says laughing.

"Girl, you're crazy!"

Mariah jumps on her bus and Janice hops in her mom's car before they drive off.

Chapter Three

Christopher turns the corner to his street and notices his mom's car is in the driveway. He walks into the house, leaving his backpack on the floor at the door.

"Hi, Mom, I'm home!" There is no answer. "Mom?" he hollers as he walks through the house. The phone rings. He walks into the kitchen to answer it but stops when he sees a note from his mother on the table. The phone continues to ring as he reads what it says. *CHRIS, I HAD TO GO ON A BUSINESS TRIP FOR A FEW DAYS. WILL BE BACK NEXT WEEK. YOUR BROTHER WILL MAKE SURE YOU GET TO SCHOOL. I'LL CALL LATER. LOVE, MOM.* Christopher shakes his head before picking up the phone.

"Hello?"

"Man, what took you so long?" Damon hollers at him from the other end of the phone.

"What do you want?"

"Can I come over and get some eggs?" Damon asks.

"Whatever, man!" Christopher says annoyed.

As soon as Christopher hangs up there is a knock at the door. He opens it after the third knock and sees Matthew standing outside. "Where is your brother?" he asks.

"I don't know. Maybe he's in his room," Christopher replies. Just then Kevin comes out and sits across the room from Matthew.

"So, what's up, White Light?" Kevin asks Matthew.

"Nothing, man," he answers. "Hey, did you see that fine new chick in school today?"

"Who?" Kevin asks.

"Her name is Jasmine. I've never talked to a black chick before, but uh, I'd talk to her!"

"Oh yeah? Well, sorry son, not before I do!" Kevin snaps back teasingly.

Christopher is still holding the phone deep in thought when there is another knock at the door. *Man, does everyone know Mom is out of town?* He opens the door. It's Damon. Damon pushes his way through and sees the other boys and pulls Christopher aside.

"So what is up with you, Man?" Damon begins to drill Christopher.

"What are you talking about? There's nothing up with me," Christopher retorts.

"Oh, come on, Dude!" Damon snaps. "I know you are all into No Brand."

"Who is No Brand?"

"You know! The one you be sitting with in Home Ec."

"You mean, Mariah?"

"Ding! Ding! Ding!" Damon shouts sarcastically.

"Why do you insist on calling her that?" Christopher asks. He's getting aggravated with Damon.

"Because, man, she never wears name brand clothes," Damon answers matter-of-factly.

"So what! I don't care about that! She's different from the other girls."

"Man, forget her! Janice is the one for you." Damon says flopping on the couch.

"Oh, so you think you know what's best for me?" Christopher asks. "Well, you don't."

"Who is No Brand?" Matthew asks.

"Some girl who has no rights to my boy's mind," Damon replies.

"Why do you call her No Brand?" Kevin asks.

"Because she doesn't wear name brand clothes, dude. Can't you hear?" Damon answers sarcastically and walks into the kitchen to head for the fridge. "Where's the eggs, Man?"

"What? You calling someone *No Brand* and you don't even have eggs? You have no eggs and you don't have any brains to find them!" Kevin retorts.

"I have eggs, man!" Damon says angrily. "I just need some extra for a project I'm working on."

"Demon hurry up and get out of here!" Kevin hollers.

"Whatever you say, Master Satan!"

Kevin throws a shoe at Damon as he walks out the door.

"Well, I'm outta here!" Matthew says as he stands up and heads for the door.

"You going to pick us up for school?" Kevin asks.

"Sure, that's cool. Just be ready. You know how you black folks are!"

"How are we?" Kevin asks angrily.

"Cool, man, and always on time!" Matthew says waving his hand to calm him down.

Mariah is lying on her back in bed, reading her Bible. She reads a passage in Isaiah 61 about receiving double for your shame. Jasmine bursts into her room.

"Girl, can't you knock?" Mariah asks.

"I can if I want to!" Jasmine answers sarcastically.

"Do it again and I will tell my momma on you," Mariah says picking her Bible up again.

"Tell! I don't care," Jasmine says as she walks out of the room and goes to put her nightclothes on. She then heads straight to the kitchen where Genevieve is cooking.

"Auntie Gen, Mariah walked in on me while I was changing my clothes," Jasmine says in a concerned, innocent voice.

"What? Mariah knows better than that!" Genevieve says irritated. She marches straight into Mariah's room. "Young lady, you know the house rules! Why, didn't you knock before entering Jasmine's room? She was changing."

"Mom, she still has her school clothes on. She was the one who walked into MY room without knocking, not me in hers!" Mariah replies all upset. Jasmine stands behind her aunt in her nightclothes to reinforce her lie.

"Mariah, you beg Jasmine's pardon right this minute!"

"But…"

"Do it now!" Genevieve hollers angrily.

"Please forgive me," Mariah whispers.

"I forgive you, but don't do it again," Jasmine says with a smile.

"Now THAT'S better!"

Genevieve walks out and returns to the kitchen, but Jasmine stays in Mariah's room. After her aunt is out of earshot, she turns to Mariah and says, "Just remember, I am smarter than you, Mariah. I am insurmountable!" Jasmine flashes Mariah a devious smile and walks out slamming the door.

Mariah slams her Bible shut and starts arguing out loud with God. With tears in her eyes she asks, "How are You going to give me double for my shame? How do You plan on doing that, God? Here I am reading Your Word, and yet You do not defend me!" Jasmine is in her room listening to Mariah and laughs. Finally, Mariah calms down and falls asleep.

Chapter Four

The morning suns shines bright on Mariah's face. She begins to stir. Noticing the sun is already up and shining, she jumps up and begins to pray. "Dear Lord, please forgive me for what I said and how I spoke to You last night," she says earnestly. "If I am not as sincere as I should be about my repentance then please help me to be more sincere each day."

Jasmine wakes up a few minutes later and hears Mariah running water in the tub. She runs in quickly and locks the door while Mariah is in her room picking out her clothes for the day. Mariah gathers her clothes together and walks to the bathroom to find the door closed.

"Is someone in there?" she asks as she turns the knob and pulls on the door. "Hello?" she says shaking the knob. Still no answer.

Mariah walks to her mom's room and knocks. "Mom, have you seen Jasmine?"

"What do you mean?" Genevieve replies as she opens the door.

"I was filling the tub up with water and went to my room to get my clothes. When I returned to the bathroom the door was locked and there was no answer," Mariah explains.

"Jasmine!" Genevieve hollers as she stands in front of the bathroom door shaking the knob.

"Just a second," Jasmine replies as she opens the door.

"What is wrong with you?" Mariah asks angrily. "I know you heard me asking if someone was in there."

"Well, she is out now, Mariah. Just go take your bath," Genevieve says.

"But Mom you don't understand. She used MY bath water that I was running!"

"Baby, just let it go," Genevieve says and begins to walk away. "I'm just glad you are both up and getting ready for school."

Mariah enters the bathroom and slams the door behind her. Genevieve turns around instantly and walks back to the bathroom door. "Open this door, young lady. Right this…" Mariah opens the door before she can finish her sentence, "minute! Have you lost your mind, little girl?" Genevieve continues. "Don't you ever disrespect me like that again! You hear me?"

"I'm sorry," she says. *You need to be that way with Jazz.*

"And you better hurry up!" her mother yells back as she walks away.

Mariah closes the door and walks over to the tub. She steps on a piece of paper as she looks down at the filthy tub. She exhales as she picks up the paper with a note from Jasmine that reads, "Ha Ha!"

"Just let it go, Mariah," she says to herself as she begins to clean the tub. "It's going to be all right."

Matthew pulls up in front of the middle school to drop Christopher off. Just as Christopher gets out, Damon walks up. "Man, I know today is going to be a good day."

"Why, cause you're going to pass your class?" Christopher teases. They laugh.

"Naw, man," Damon says rubbing his hands together. "I just feel like something exciting is going to happen today."

"How do you know?"

"Because I am SPEAKING it!" Damon says with an ornery grin.

"Oh, so now you know the Bible, do you?"

"Well, yeah, I do know a little something," Damon says.

As they enter into the school, some girls walk by and say hi to Chris. "Hi, Ladies!" Christopher replies back with a handsome grin.

"Ladies? Those aren't ladies. You should say, 'Hi, Easy!'" Damon says insulting the girls. One of the girls raises her middle finger to Damon as they walk off with angry looks on their faces.

Damon shouts another insult out and one of the girls stops and turns around flashing him a dirty look. "What did you just say to me?" she asks.

"I wasn't talking to you!" Damon replies.

"Yes, you were. I know what I heard and I know whose mouth was moving," she says, putting her hands on her hips. "Wait a minute! I know who you are. You must be the one all the girls are talking about."

"Oh, you mean the one that can bust a move?" he brags. The boys in the hall start to laugh.

"No. The one they call "Waterbed." Everyone laughs at that including teachers who were standing nearby. Everyone except Damon.

"Well, if I was ever in question about whether or not you knew God, I sure have my answer now!" Christopher says, turning to look at Damon.

"What do you mean? What are you talking about?"

"I mean it is obvious that you know some of the Bible, but you do not follow through with what it says."

"Whatever, man! Why do you laugh at me?" Damon asks.

"Because you are a fool, man. That was God chastising you for treating those girls the way you did."

Bernice Whitman, a devout wife and C.E.O. of the family. She makes sure that everyone in her family has everything they need to maintain their success, until one morning she is faced with an unknown routine that catches her by surprise. Bernice suddenly wakes up and realizes she is going to be late getting her son, Samuel, to school. She looks over and sees her husband standing in front of the mirror straightening his tie. "David, why didn't you wake me up?" she asks him, frantically jumping out of bed.

"I told you, darling. Samuel is your problem, not mine," he replies as he reaches for his suit coat.

Bernice throws on her clothes and runs to Samuel's room. She enters and finds candy and Twinkie wrappers all over the floor with empty soda cans strewn here and there. She shakes Samuel, who is sound asleep still. "Look at this room! Samuel, wake up!" she yells.

"Wha…huh?" he says still groggy.

"Get up!" she yells and begins picking up trash. "Get up now. You're late for school. Hurry and get dressed. This room looks like a pig's sty."

Bernice goes down to the kitchen and begins making toast and jam with a glass of orange juice for Samuel. David comes into the kitchen with his briefcase and kisses his wife's face. He notices there is only one glass of juice and one piece of toast made.

"Just give up on him," he says shaking his head. "He's old enough to get himself up. He needs to learn responsibility. You care more about his things than he does!"

"I don't think he deserves BOTH parents feeling that way," she says.

David picks up the toast and drinks the juice. "I'm stress free! Can you say that?" he asks as he turns to walk out of the kitchen. "I'll call you later. By the way, thanks for the toast!"

Samuel walks in ready to leave for school. "Put your shirt inside your pants, young man," she asks angrily while shaking him. "How many times do I have to tell you to look at yourself in the mirror when you finish dressing?"

"I can't help it!" Samuel yells. "I come from a pig sty, remember?" He runs off toward his room.

"Samuel, wait! I didn't mean it like that!" Bernice hollers.

"Leave me alone!" Samuel yells as he runs in his room and slams the door.

"I am sorry, Samuel. I didn't mean it like that. Please, let's talk," Bernice pleads outside his door.

"No, leave me alone. I'm never coming out!"

"Please, let's talk," Bernice asks again but with no response. She slides down the wall, setting her back against it. "Ok, then just come out whenever you are ready. I will call the school."

Samuel pulls a box of pie out from under his bed. He opens it and begins eating it. The rest of the pie he throws at the wall. He falls to his knees. "I don't want to be like this anymore," he cries and hides his head in his hands.

"Lord, please help us!" Bernice cries.

Class has already begun and everyone in Home Economics class is whisking the eggs in their bowls. Candace approaches Miss Louivere. "Miss Lou, Samuel is not here and I'm not sure what I am supposed to do without a partner."

"Does anyone know why Samuel is not here?" she asks.

"Who is that?" several students in the class ask.

"He's the young man who sits with Candace," Miss Lou replies.

"Oh, you mean, Big Drawls?" Damon says sarcastically.

"No name calling in this class, and be advised that this is your LAST warning!" Miss Lou says sharply.

"Well, I'd call the offices if I was the teacher," Candace suggests.

"I am always glad to see a student figuring out the teacher's problem even when she can't figure out her own," Miss Lou says to Candace. "I'm pretty sure you can handle this situation all by yourself, Candace. After all, it's only eggs."

Rodney is in the bathroom bent over and wiping mud off of his shoes. Anthony walks in and notices bruises on Rodney's back.

"Hey, dude. Next time you buy shoes, get some without strings. You're too tall for bending over to lace them," Anthony says jokingly, trying not to let Rodney know he saw the bruises.

Rodney stands up immediately and pulls his shirt down to make sure no one sees. Anthony goes over to use the urinal.

"So what are you doing this weekend?" Rodney asks Anthony.

"I have no idea," Anthony says as he goes to the sink and begins washing his hands. "By the way, how's your mom?"

"Not good," he answers sadly. "Not good at all."

"Sorry to hear that," Anthony says. "So what about your dad? Is he still crazy?"

"As life itself!" Rodney replies.

"Hey, if you ever need to talk, I'm here. So later! I'm getting out of here before the teacher comes in!"

Back in Home Economics class Mariah and Christopher are standing at the stove frying their eggs. The others have not yet finished mixing all of their ingredients. Christopher looks down at Mariah. "So, do you know what you are doing?"

"Yes, of course I do. I make eggs for my family all the time," she says.

"Well, then, why don't you let me fry the eggs since you already know what you are doing? I need a good grade in this class," Christopher suggests. Mariah steps aside and motions for him to take over.

"One day I hope you'll let me cook breakfast for you," he says staring at the eggs in the pan. Mariah smiles.

"Well, what do you say?" he asks looking at her now.

"Well, I don't know."

Janice notices how close Christopher and Mariah are and is not happy about it. Neither is Damon. "Miss Lou, can we be next?" Damon asks.

"Well, if you're ready then get in line," she says.

Mariah goes and sits down at her desk and waits for Christopher to bring the finished project back to the table. Damon moves in behind Mariah with his bowl of eggs and bends down to whisper to her. "So, I hear you know how to cook." Janice sees a perfect opportunity to humiliate Mariah. She jumps up out of her chair and bumps into Damon, knocking the bowl of scrambled eggs out of his hand and onto Mariah's head and clothes. The other students laugh.

"Oh, Mariah, I didn't mean to do that!" Damon immediately says.

As the eggs roll down her head and onto her face, Mariah tries to wipe the ingredients out of her eyes in order to search for the room's exit. She needs an escape from the extreme humiliation. Miss Lou and Christopher run to Mariah with paper towels and help wipe her face.

"Man, why did you have to do that for?" Christopher asks Damon angrily.

"I hate this school!" Mariah shouts as she runs out the door to the bathroom.

"Mr. Damon Lewis, report to the principal's office this instant!" Miss Lou shouts.

Damon gathers his backpack up. He knew there was no need in arguing.

"How could you do that to her?" Christopher asks Damon. "So, I guess that is why you needed all those eggs from my house." Damon is speechless. "Answer me, Damon!"

"I can't," Damon whispers as he walks out the door.

Janice gathers Mariah's things and takes them to the bathroom. Candace sees the whole thing and just lays her head down on the table.

Mariah is in the bathroom splashing water on her face when Janice walks in. Janice grabs some paper towels and hands them to her.

"Is there something that wrong with me, Janice? Why do people want to put me down all the time?" Mariah asks with tears in her eyes. "I go home and it's a problem. I come to school and it is even more of a problem." She pauses to dry her face and wipe her eyes. "I wear decent clothes. No, they are not name brand, but…never mind. This is just too much."

"Christopher should have helped you," Janice says finally.

"What?"

"Doesn't he like you?" Janice asks, baiting her.

"I'm here spilling my heart out to you in tears and all you do is talk about Chris?"

"I'm just saying…"

"Saying what? That you like him?" Mariah asks angrily.

"Girl, please! It was probably all just a big set up. You know, all those extra eggs Damon had."

Just then the teacher walks in.

"Mariah, go down to the office and call your parents to pick you up," Miss Lou says. Just then more girls walk into the bathroom. "What happened to her?" they ask.

As Mariah walks down the hall in front of all her peers, she hears the comments and noises they make that humiliate her even more. Totally disgraced, she uses the office phone to call home. Damon comes out of the principal's office and sees Mariah. He genuinely feels bad for her and puts his head down as he walks by to the counselor's office. He hears Mariah talking to her mom.

"I don't know, Momma. Can't you just come get me?" she pleads.

"Mariah, school is almost out. Can't you just wait there and ride the bus home?" Genevieve asks over the phone.

"Momma no," Mariah says as tears fill her eyes. "Please, Momma. Please come."

Damon knocks on the door of Mrs. Geo's office. The counselor asks him to be seated.

"Damon Lewis, what seems to be the problem?" she asks.

"I don't want to talk about it," he replies with his head down.

"And why not?"

"I am suspended already. This whole thing is completely out of order. I thought I was supposed to come here first and then the office. This school is backwards!" he says just rambling on.

"Why are you suspended?"

"I'm not talking to you," he says sarcastically.

"I have news for you. You WILL talk to me and you can start by telling me how long you are going to be out of school."

"Long enough not to learn anything else in class."

"Like what?" she asks.

"Like EGGS, EGGS and more EGGS!" he yells.

"Oh, so you were in Home Economics. So how many days will you be out of class?"

"Can I just go now?"

"Before you do, remember this. No one gets away with anything. You need to learn wisdom. Wisdom will cause you to think twice and speak once. It will also help you to think about your future. Remember, your words create your destiny. It's all about choices." She leans back in her chair. "You may leave now."

Mrs. Geo walks to the Home Economics room and knocks on the door. Miss Lou opens it. "May I have a word with you?" she asks Miss Lou.

"Sure, what seems to be the problem?"

"I need to know if anything unusual happened in class today," Mrs. Geo inquired.

"Well, yes, there was an incident. Damon Lewis spilled eggs all over a young lady. My God, she was practically covered from head to toe!"

"Was it on purpose?" Mrs. Geo asks.

"I am not for sure if it was, but I know that this young man has been nothing but trouble from the very beginning."

"Did the girl go home?"

"I don't know. I hope someone came and picked her up so she didn't have to ride the bus with those cruel peers of hers," Miss Lou replied.

"Yes, let's hope! Thanks, Miss Lou."

Mariah hid until it was time to catch the bus. She runs towards it the second she sees it coming.

Candace sees her and tries to talk with her. "Mariah, wait! I need to talk to you."

"For what, Candace? Look at me! I just want to get home." Mariah doesn't stop but keeps aiming for the bus.

"But I have something to tell you!"

"What now?"

"It's important. Can I call you?" Candace pleads. "Please give me your number."

"All right. 555-6012."

"Thanks!" Candace says and turns away as Mariah gets on the bus. She sees Janice staring at her.

As Mariah takes her seat on the bus she begins to pray to herself. *God, please don't let them start harassing me.*

One of the boys on the bus hollers at her. "Ewww. What's that on your shirt? Snot?" The other children on the bus start laughing. Mariah has tears in her eyes. "How did you get snot all over you?"

"It's not snot! It's eggs!" she cries.

"Look, it's all in her hair," he says and starts to sing a song about it. "*Oh, my God! There's eggs everywhere. My momma won't come get me, so I fry 'em in my hair! I fry 'em in my hair!*" The children on the bus laughed even harder.

Chapter Five

Mariah runs into the house and goes straight to her room. She falls onto her bed and begins to cry. Her mom is in the living room talking to her dad. "I should've gone and picked her up. God only knows what happened on that bus today," Genevieve says to her husband Allen.

"No, you did right," he replies. "We only pick up people when they make the Honor Roll."

"That's our daughter. How can you say that?"

"Look, I'd be concerned if it was Jasmine. That girl makes the Honor Roll. I'd pick her up any day."

"That's not fair, Allen! How are we going to neglect our child and support someone else?" Genevieve asks.

"Genevieve, now I told you I didn't want her in the first place. You shouldn't be surprised by my attitude. You know how I have felt about her from the day she was born," Allen says nonchalantly.

"You better be careful what you say. God is listening!" Genevieve shouts at him angrily.

"Well, I'm glad somebody is! If you would have listened to me you would have given her away!"

"You watch your mouth, man!"

"I have spoken and you need to heed my advice, woman."

"Hey, Uncle Allen and Auntie Gen, can I go hang out with my friends?"

"Are you an Honor Student?" Allen asks her.

"But of course!" Jasmine answers with a grin.

"Then be back before midnight."

Genevieve glares at Allen, but before she can say anything he says, "I don't want to hear it. You already know how I feel."

"Jasmine, do you want anything to eat before you go?" Genevieve asks.

"No, I will pick something up later," she replies as she runs out the door.

A few minutes later, Mariah comes down and goes into the kitchen to get a drink. "Mariah, are you ready to eat?" her mom asks her.

"No, thanks. I'm not hungry."

"Good! More for me then!" her father says sarcastically.

Mariah finishes her drink and returns to her room. She picks up her headset and begins listening to some

Gospel music. She gets lost in the music and little by little the events of the day begin to fade away.

A few hours later Jasmine comes in and slowly cracks open the door. She sees Mariah lying on her bed with her headphones on and her eyes closed. She shuts the door and goes into her room to get ready for bed. Mariah finishes with her music and lays her headset on the floor before she begins to pray.

"Father, please help me to be kind to others, regardless of how they treat me. It gets so hard sometimes, but Jesus, You are my Rock and You never change. You care about me and I thank You for that. Lord, You saw what happened today. No one cared. No one gave me a hug. No one even asked if I was ok or how I was doing. Jesus, it hurt so badly. I don't know how much more I can take, but I know You do. I don't really want to know how much more I can handle, but I ask this one request. Please send a caring heart or a kind word. In Jesus' Name. Amen!" Mariah shuts her eyes and soon drifts off to sleep.

Jasmine gets up in the middle of the night to use the bathroom. On her way back to her room, she wonders what Mariah was listening to earlier on her headset. She doesn't have a headset as nice as Mariah's. She decides that she wants it for herself. Jasmine sneaks into Mariah's room while she's sleeping and tiptoes over to the headset on the floor. She places the headset over her ears and listens to what's playing. It's gospel music. Jasmine smirks. Instead of stealing the headset, she chooses to pull a prank. She takes Mariah's headphones and fills them up with baby oil. She puts them back on the floor where they were and goes back to bed.

The next morning Mariah is in the living room watching television when the phone rings. Her momma hollers at her from the other room, "Mariah, pick up the phone!"

"Ok, got it!" she says picking up the phone. "Hello?" she says into the receiver.

"Hey!" said the voice on the other end.

"Who is this?" Mariah asks.

"It's Candace."

"Oh, hi. How's it going?"

"I wanted to know if you could meet me at the library?" Candace asks.

"I, uh…I guess," Mariah says slowly, thinking about it for a moment.

"Ok, meet me there in ten minutes," Candace says.

"Ok." They say goodbye and hang up.

Mariah walks into the kitchen where her mom and dad are talking at the table. "Mom, can I go to the library?"

"What for? You can't read. The teachers just pass you so you can stay stupid," her father snips.

"Baby, go on. Don't listen to him."

"I won't, Momma. Thanks!" Mariah says as she kisses her mom on the cheek and walks out.

Candace and Mariah are sitting in the library talking. "Do you come here often?" Mariah asks.

"Yes, I sure do. This is the only place where it is quiet. Nobody can mess with you here," Candace replies.

"What? You have people that pick on you?'

"Yes. Girls at my church and neighbors."

"What kind of things do they say?" Mariah asks curiously.

"They make fun of me because of the way I dress. My mom makes me wear these hats like the other women she knows in her group. I don't like wearing the hats and getting made fun of."

"What? That's it?" Mariah asks.

"Yes. Basically."

"I'd go through that with a smile!" Mariah says matter-of-factly.

"Mariah, you're missing the point."

"Well, please inform me," she says.

"Being somewhere where you are different can be uncomfortable. People reject what is different," Candace explains.

"I know. I can relate to that! So why did you want me to come here?"

"I wanted to talk to you about yesterday."

"What about it?" Mariah questions.

"I saw what happened."

"Yes, of course you did. Everyone saw what Damon did!"

"No, it was an accident," Candace says.

"That wasn't an accident!" Mariah snaps back. "Damon did it on purpose!"

"I think you're wrong. He may have thought about it, but he had help."

"Help? From who?" Mariah asks curiously.

"From Janice."

"Janice? No, she's my friend," Mariah retorts.

"Trust me, she is NOT your friend."

"How would YOU know?" Mariah questions angrily.

"Because, I've been watching her."

"What? You're my secret agent now?"

"No, Mariah, you just need to stop being so gullible!"

A librarian walks in and says, "Please lower your voices in here, ladies. Better yet, let's close the door."

"Ok, go on," Mariah says to Candace.

"You need to start paying attention. That girl is jealous of you."

"Jealous? Of what?"

"Well, for one…Christopher and the other. Take a look in the mirror!"

Mariah pauses for a moment to think about what Candace has said. "And why do you care?"

"I don't know, but I do know this. If you really are "a nobody" then no one has anything to say to you. Think about it. If there is nothing there, how can you discover it?"

Mariah looks up from their discussion and sees Samuel looking for a book. "Hey, that looks like Samuel. Does he come here too?"

"I don't know. I've never seen him here before."

Mariah gets up and goes over to Samuel. Candace follows.

"Hi, Samuel!" Mariah says quietly. Samuel doesn't answer.

"Come on, Samuel. You hear us talking to you. Now answer us!" Candace says a little louder.

"What?" Samuel finally says.

"Why didn't you come to school yesterday?" Mariah asks.

"Yeah, I had to mix and cook the eggs all by myself," Candace adds teasingly.

Mariah notices Samuel's dirty, torn clothes and his busted lip. "What happened to your clothes?" Mariah asks.

"Yeah, and your mouth?" Candace adds.

"Some guys were calling me bad names after I left the snow-ball stand. They started chasing me and I fell."

"What's sno-ball stand?" Candace asks.

"You never had a snow-ball?" Mariah asks. "My mom won't let me have boudin either."

"Don't tell me you don't know what that is?" asked Samuel.

"Of course I know. It's rice dressing stuffed inside of pork skin."

"That is called casing, as far as the rice dressing..... you're pretty close but you have to look that up for yourself. To sum it all up, it's basically a pork sauage." Mariah adds.

"Well, what about the sno-ball?"

"It's shaved ice with your favorite flavored syrup that comes in different flavors like watermelon, pac-man, wedding cake. The list goes on," says Samuel.

"I still don't understand why your mom keeps you away from something that is a part of our culture," Mariah says confoundedly.

"Mom always told me, what's good for the sugar is bad for the salt." Mariah and Samuel look at each other more confused than ever.

"It means, if it's good for the taste it's bad for your waist."

Everybody laughs!

"Why did they do that?" Mariah asks with genuine concern.

"I don't know. Probably because I'm fat. They called me hog-head cheese and I called them red throat."

"Red throat?" Mariah asks puzzled.

"What's that?" Candace asks.

"I don't know it's the only thing that I could think of at the time. I guess it is somebody with an infection in their mouth."

They laughed.

The librarian comes over. "I'm sorry, but I am going to have to ask you to leave. Quietly please. Try again next week."

Chapter Six

Bernice is busy working around her house when suddenly she realizes she has not seen Samuel in a while. She frantically looks around for him and enters the hall so she can knock on his bedroom door. No answer. She opens the door, almost afraid of what she might find. Nothing. He is not there. She is now about to have an anxiety attack. She picks up the phone and dials Matthew. "Do you know where your brother is?"

"No, I have no idea, but he probably is somewhere eating," he says sarcastically.

Bernice is worried and doesn't know what to do. She sits down at the table and pours herself some juice. She has been sitting there worried and waiting for quite some time when finally Samuel walks in the door with a couple of books in his hands. Bernice is now sitting in the dark where Samuel can't see her.

"Where have you been?" she asks frantically.

Samuel is startled. "With some friends."

"Friends? What friends? You have friends?"

"Yes, I do." He smiles as he says that.

"Boys? Girls?" his mother asks, drilling him.

"Girls. BEAUTIFUL girls!" he replies grinning from ear to ear.

Bernice sees his smile and relaxes. She is elated by his response, seeing the look on her son's face. "Well, that is great to hear, but leave a note next time, will ya?"

It's late evening and Rodney's dad is already hammered. Rodney's dad had owned a club but he ended up losing it because he was drinking too much of his own product. When the customers would come, the majority of the liquor was half way gone. Eventually he stopped but after his wife became ill, he started drinking again. In a drunken rage, Eddie rips the thermostat off the wall and trips over the box fan, busting it to pieces. He starts throwing things all over the house. When Rodney comes down to see what's going on, Eddie begins beating him for disrespecting him. Rodney's mom, Mrs. Edna, has been a nurse until she became ill six years ago. Today she is in her room with her breathing machine on. She's weak and sweaty without any air-conditioning or fans in her room. She hears the commotion, removes her oxygen and slowly staggers out to the living room.

"Get out of my house, you good for nothing!" Eddie screams at Rodney.

"Stop it! Just stop it!" Edna shouts as loud as she can at Eddie.

"You see my mom is sick and you don't even care!" Rodney hollers at his dad.

Eddie smacks Rodney across the face, knocking him to the floor. He kicks him while he is down. "Stop it! Eddie, I said stop! Calm down!" Edna shouts.

"I am calm, woman!"

"Baby, go to your room. Let me talk to your daddy."

"But Momma I don't…"

"Just go. Please baby. Go," Edna says with tears in her eyes.

Rodney gets up off the floor and touches his mother's cheek as he walks by. He goes to his room, throws himself on his bed and sobs.

"Now you listen here to me, Eddie. You listen good. Pastor Rhine always said the more you drink of that devil juice the crazier you get."

"I can't help it!"

"Oh yes you can. You just have to fight it. You beat your own son because that alcohol is beating you. It is controlling you. There is going to be a winner. I just hope it is you," she says as she throws the bottle of alcohol in the trash after dumping it out in the sink. "I need you to get better, Eddie. I don't know how much longer I'm going to be here."

"Woman, why you talk like that?"

"Because it's true."

Rodney has come out of his room and is sitting at the top of the steps, listening with tears running down his bruised face.

"It is time to be a man and get your house in order."

"You're saying I'm not a man?" Eddie asks.

"What man do you see walking around throwing temper tantrums? Only little boys do that. Men are supposed to be in charge, not out of control. Understand this, Eddie. Anger lies in the bosom of fools. No strong man can come destroy the house of a wise owner."

"You calling alcohol the strong man?" he says, glancing down at his clenched fists.

"Yes, you are the owner. You bought it, didn't you?"

"I sure did!" he says gloating.

"Next time...DON'T!" she says as she turns and stumbles back to her room.

Mariah's family walks in to their house from church. Genevieve walks in humming a hymn, removes her hat and sits it on the table. Mariah is dressed in her Sunday best. She's humming also, so full of joy.

"Church was awesome this morning, huh, Momma?"

"It sure was, dear!"

"It was ok, but why they have to keep people there so long?" Jasmine says whining.

"Rest assured, it wasn't as long as you hanging out with your friends all night. Now set the table," Genevieve says flashing her niece an aggravated look.

Mariah goes to her room and changes her clothes. She grabs her CD player and lays herself across her bed. It doesn't work so she opens it up to see why. It is full of oil. She smells it and realizes it is baby oil. "What in the name of…?" She's enraged and storms to the kitchen. Jasmine's back is turned and doesn't know Mariah is coming at her. Mariah forcefully pushes her to the ground.

"Why? Why do you continue to do horrible things to me? Why Jasmine, why? Now stand up!"

"What are you talking about?" Jasmine tries to say innocently for her aunt's sake.

Genevieve hears the commotion and comes into the kitchen. "What is going on in here?"

"Jasmine destroyed my CD player!"

"I didn't do anything!" Jasmine shouts.

"What? Let me see," Genevieve says as she takes the player from Mariah. She opens it and sees the oil. She smells it too. "Is this baby oil?"

"It sure is!" Mariah says.

"Jasmine, did you do this?" Genevieve angrily asks, glaring at Jasmine.

"Well, I uh…"

"Well, what?"

"I was only joking. It was supposed to be a joke and…"

"Well, you forgot to laugh! It was no joke!" Mariah says angrily.

"You are slipping, Mariah." Jasmine sneers.

"What do you mean?"

"I thought you are supposed to spend time with God without ceasing? I did that yesterday."

"How dare you change the subject? This is about you. Not me! Besides, it's because of HIM that I have not killed you in your sleep!" Mariah turns and stomps off to her room and slams the door.

"Auntie, are you going to let her talk to me like that?" Jasmine asks trying to be all hurt.

"Jasmine just stop! Didn't you hear her? Jesus is the reason you are still here."

A little while later Genevieve goes into Mariah's room. "Are you ready to eat?"

"No, I'm not hungry."

"How can you not be hungry? You haven't eaten anything."

"I just don't want to eat, Momma."

"Is it because of Jasmine?" Jasmine is eavesdropping outside the door. "Baby, you should not let anyone take away your joy. This body right here," she says tapping

Mariah's belly, "needs to be fed. No one, I mean NO ONE, should have that much power over you to make you stop treating yourself right."

"I know, it's just that there is so much that she says and does that nobody sees or hears."

"So, you're calling your BIG DADDY GOD nobody?"

"No, of course not. I mean people on earth."

"Mariah, no one should matter but God. Don't put your confidence in men, only in Jesus. You know the Word. 'If God be for you...'"

"Who can be against you?"

"That's my girl! Now, let's go get something to eat." Jasmine quickly moves away from the door.

Later during the day, Mariah is sitting in her bedroom reading a book about leadership.

Her mom slightly opens her door and asks, "Is it okay to come in?" Mariah nods before Genevieve steps inside. "What are you reading?"

"A book on how to become a leader."

"What caused you to look into that?"

"My goal in life is to be a leader for young children."

"So you want to be a teacher or some sort?" Genevieve asks.

"I don't know, maybe. All I know is that I have a lot of time on my hands, and I wanted to use it by preparing for my expected future. Also, I can get familiar with my future career."

"I'm so proud of you," say Genevieve with a smile.

"Thanks Mom. I really needed to hear that."

Genevieve was going to talk to Mariah about something important but holds back, not wanting to lose Mariah's focus. She decides to discuss it later while heading for the door. Before she leaving she glances back at her beautiful daughter and says, "By the way, there's something I would like to share with you later."

Mariah raises her brow and closes her book. "We can talk now.?

"Are you sure?

"Yeah, why not?"

Genevieve quietly nods and looks down at the floor. "How about we take a walk outside?"

It's been a while since the two of them shared private time together, so Mariah is elated to go on a walk with her mom. She puts her paperwork in a safe place and heads outside her room, holding her mom's hand.

Walking in the grass outside the house, Genevieve begins to tell her daughter what's been gnawing at her. "You know, when my sister asked me to have Jasmine live with us I didn't know how to feel or respond. So many thoughts were running through my head. All I could think about was how selfish my sister was being. She couldn't manage to fit her own daughter into her life. She's so invested in herself and doesn't care about anyone else. Especially Jasmine. But then I thought about you and how nice it would be for you to have someone to grow up with. With that in mind, I agreed to do it. My sister told me that she'd send a thousand dollars a month for taking her in but that she wanted me to make sure Jasmine didn't want for nothing. I tried to keep her promise. And now this whole time that Jasmine's been here I've neglected you. I could've bought you the same things as her. I could've spent more time with you. Instead, I was busy worrying about Jasmine and making sure she didn't feel ostracized."

As they continue to walk, Mr. Allen passes by the window, wondering what they are talking about.

Still talking with her daughter, Genevieve hangs her head low in shame. "I may not have much money as my sister does, but I feel guilty for not being there for you. I guess that's why God said to take the beam out your own eye first."

"Mom! It's okay. Everything happens for a reason," says Mariah.

"Well, with that being said, I wanted to share something else with you. Something no one knows. Not even your father." Genevieve tries her hardest to keep strong in front of Mariah, but she can't hide the sadness from her eyes.

"What's going on?" Mariah asks.

"I'm really sick," Genevieve finally says.

Mariah's quiet for a moment, raking it all in. "What do you mean? You have cancer?"

"No. I have Lupus."

"Is that like a skin disease?

Genevieve hesitantly responds.

"It's more serious than that."

"What? What exactly are you trying to tell me…"

"I'm saying that it's been affecting my brain and kidneys. The day you called from school I had just gotten back from the hospital. I had a seizure."

Mariah's eyes widened from shock. "Why didn't you say anything then! And why are we standing out here in the sun?" She takes her mom's hand and tries to lead her to the house.

Genevieve grabs a hold of her little girl's arms to stop her. "Baby! The damage has been done."

"The damage has been done? You're saying that you're about to die." Tears immediately begin to fill her eyes. "You're telling me that you're about to leave me and that I'm not going to have a mother anymore? I'm not accepting this. You are going to live a long and happy life."

Mariah drops to her knees and starts sobbing in her hands.

Genevieve reaches for her daughter and hugs her from behind. Mariah pulls herself together and turns around to hug her mother.

"I'm sharing this with you now because I know that you are strong in the Lord and you can handle this," Genevieve says.

"I love you, Mom." Mariah whispers.

"I love you more."

"Whatever God's will is, I'll accept it through his strength."

Mariah walks her mom inside the house. As soon as they enter, Mr. Allen says, "Ya'll was crying out there like somebody is dying."

Chapter Seven

Months later, it is now the last week of school. The students are all in their seats in Miss Lou's Home Economics class.

"Well students, the year is almost over, and I must say this has been one of my most interesting classes. Some of you have done an excellent job and some, well, not so excellent. So those of you who have already passed my class do not have to take the final. Good luck to those of you who do!"

"What's it going to be about? Eggs?" Damon says with a grin, looking around to see who is laughing. No one laughs.

"Damon, perhaps I should fail you for your acts of rebellion."

"What? Rebellion?"

"Yes, look it up. You do own a dictionary, don't you?" Students laugh.

While Miss Lou is getting onto Damon, Christopher is talking to Mariah sitting next to him. "Why have you been playing hard to get?"

"Chris, I told you. I don't want a boyfriend right now. Especially not while I am in school."

"Are you sure about that?" he asks with a deep sigh.

"Absolutely!"

"Then don't get upset when I get a girl in high school."

"I'll help you get her!" Mariah said with a grin.

"Whatever."

Miss Lou turns to the rest of the class. "Those of you who have passed my class, today is your last day. You do not have to come in tomorrow. Thank you for doing your part. You are well on your way to success. You are dismissed. The rest of you remain for instructions on tomorrow's final."

Candace and Mariah are walking together in the hallway. They pass by some girls standing around talking. They see Janice who is bent over the fountain getting a drink of water. "So, Mariah, you want to hang out tomorrow?" Candace asks.

"Sure, why not. What will we do this time? And don't say the library!" she says chuckling.

"Oh, I'll think of something," Candace replies laughing.

"Excuse me. What are the two of you talking about?" Janice interrupts.

"Mariah, I'll call you later," Candace says as she flashes Janice a look and walks out of the school building.

"Hold, on a minute. Did I just miss something here?" Janice asks. Mariah ignores her and keeps walking.

"Mariah, I said wait! Are you and Candace hanging out together now, and phoning each other?"

"Yes, she is a good person. You and I never hung out before," Mariah finally answers.

"How can you say that?" Janice asks. I was just about to ask you if you wanted a ride home."

"Oh, that's it?"

"Well, no. Before we took you home, I was going to see if you wanted to go to the park." Mariah was not convinced she was telling the truth. "So, do you want to or not?"

"Sure, I guess." Mariah leaves with Janice and her mom. As they drive off, the bell rings.

Mariah and Janice are sitting at a picnic table under the veranda at the park. "Why do you not want to talk to Chris anymore?" Janice asks as she sits on the table, looking down at Mariah.

"I have better things to do with my time than that right now."

"Don't you think he is cute and sexy?" Janice asks.

"Yes, all of the above, but I'm just not ready for a boyfriend."

"Well, I am! Everybody else is doing it," Janice says. "Sometimes it's just that I get bored. You know, my mom works so much and can't take me anywhere."

"I have a one track mind right now, Janice, and it does not include a boyfriend or sex."

"Well, you need to do it. Then maybe those boys will quit harassing you."

"That's not true," Mariah retorts.

"Well, how do you know if you don't try it and find out?"

"Because I don't want to find out. I have standards and morals."

"Are you saying you're still a virgin?"

"And you're NOT?"

"Girl, please! Some things you just can't resist!" Janice says grinning. "You are my girl and all, Mariah, but you are slow!"

"And you are too fast, Janice. Besides, what's the point of having sex with someone you don't know anything about? Someone whose parents are still taking care of them?"

"Well, that's why you get to know them."

"Janice, the majority of them can't even fry eggs!" They both laugh.

"You have a good point, but it doesn't make any sense to stop now."

"Yes, it does. Just because you make one bad choice, doesn't mean you keep making them."

"I don't think I am that strong," Janice says regretfully.

"When you meet the right one and can't get rid of the diseases from all of the wrong ones, you are going to look back and see how strong you could have been. You should try to make better choices now while you have a chance."

Janice's mom blows the car horn. Sticking her head out the window, she hollers, "Come on, girls. I have to go to work!"

"Thanks for the outing, Janice. I can't remember the last time I was here," Mariah says as they walk towards the car. A few minutes later, Janice's mom pulls up in front of Mariah's house.

"Thanks, Ms. Brenda!" Mariah says as she gets out of the car.

"Any time!" Brenda replies with a smile.

"Bye, girl! I'll see you later," Janice says, waving to Mariah.

Mariah enters her house and finds it dark and quiet. "Hello? Anybody home?" There is no answer. She goes to her room and flops down on the bed. She begins to pray. "Well, Jesus, my friend. I thank you for helping me pass my classes. I pray for those who did not. Also, Lord, I pray that in my high school years a new rule is passed that all parishes have to wear uniforms. If not all of them, at least mine. If it be Your will, in Jesus' Name!"

Mariah gets up and notices there is a gift on the floor. She opens it and finds a new CD player with a new CD inside. As she presses play, she lies down and begins listening to the song, "I Will Blessed The Lord" by Anna B. She soon drifts off to sleep.

Days go by and Mariah has to adjust with Jasmine attending school with her, since Mariah has to be more careful now than ever. One day in class, Jasmine starts talking to the classmates around her desk, and starts spreading lies about Mariah. Even though this happened months ago, Jasmine tells the story as if it just happened. Not only that, but she plays the victim and turns the story around.

"So, the other day after church I was going listen to the *Shy* CD, but when I opened my CD player it was filled with baby oil. Then before I know it, Mariah went and told her mother that I was the one that did that to her instead. I just can't take it anymore!"

"What did her mom do?" asked one of the classmates.

"She believed her," Jasmine says, wiping fake tears from her face.

"That doesn't make sense to me. It sounds childish," says another classmate.

Jasmine sniffs and continues telling her story. "After that, I went to my room and found a note that Mariah left. It said that I'm too dark to be related to her."

"Are you serious?" someone asks.

"That's not cool!" shouts a classmate at the back of the room. Everyone starts feeling sorry for Jasmine, all the while judging Mariah for her actions.

Another student hands Jasmine a tissue and asks, "Did Mariah apologize to you this morning?"

Jasmine shakes her head. "She just called me dark and ugly."

"And to think, I thought she was this beautiful, sweet, quiet girl," someone says.

Jasmine dabs the tissue under her wet eyes. "She's quiet all right. She was 6 years old doing different types of nasty things with boys."

When the bell rings, everyone races out of the classroom. Mariah walks down the hallway with her new name brand clothes. She smiles down the hallway, feeling like a new person.

Rodney passes by her and yells, "IT'S ABOUT TIME!"

Mariah pays him no mind. As she walks to the restroom, a group from Jasmine's class follows her inside.

When she turns to the bathroom stall, the girls come out from behind and attack her. They blindfold her, ignoring Mariah's screams.

"Stop! Why are you doing this to me?"

To prevent Mariah from screaming, they force some paper towels in her mouth. They stretch her legs out, tugging her in opposite directions as if she were a wishbone. The girls tie up her hands while someone is guarding the door. "Make sure you don't hit her in the face so no can believe her," one of the girls orders.

They repeatedly stomp and hit her in the stomach. They start kicking her so hard she wets her new clothes.

As soon as the bell rings, the girls leave Mariah on the floor and exit the restroom.

Humiliated and embarrassed, Mariah pushes herself up and pulls down the scarf that kept her from seeing. She manages to wiggle her hands lose from their ties and removes the paper towels from her mouth. She looks at her reflection in the mirror, trying to put her hair back in place but she just can barely move. The pain in her arm feels like a train just rolled over them.

Mariah cries out, "WHY ME? WHY ME? WHY? WHY?" At that moment, a teacher walking by the bathroom hears her outburst and comes to her rescue.

Mariah is given a couple of days off from school. Her best friends, Candace and Samuel, find out who attacked her and the principal had them expelled.

When it's time to go back Mariah never does. After everything that happened at school, Jasmine could no longer remain in the same house as Mariah. She was sent back home to be with her mom overseas.

Chapter Eight

As time passes a lot of things have changed and are changing, some for the better and others for the worse.

Mariah is about to graduate from college in a few days with a PhD in psychology. She has already obtained her Master's in Education and Business. Every day, whether she has classes or not, she visits her mom at the hospital. On occasion, she visits her father in the nursing home.

Mariah is turning in the parking lot of the hospital to visit her mom. The hospital is under construction. Tony, the supervisor over the project, has been interested in Mariah since the first time she went to the hospital. He wasn't sure how to approach her to ask her out. When he did, she said yes. The two have be dating for a while.

He also spends time at Mrs. Genevieve's bedside since he knows that Mariah visits her mother daily.

Tony is tall, beautiful skin tone, sexy with a perfect smile. Tony Lewis Chen was adopted when he was seven years old by an Asian man and a black woman. They allowed him to keep his last name but uses it for his middle name since he didn't have one.

"When will you ask my daughter out again?" asks Mrs. Genevieve.

"I plan to do that today sometime today," says Tony, with a chuckle.

"Tell me again," Mrs. Genevieve coughs, then continues, "about the first time you saw my child."

Tony reflects, "The sun was so bright outside that day. I knew something special was coming my way. And there she was pulling up in the parking lot. As she shut the door to her car, she was in such a rush. She mistakenly closed part of her dress in the car door. I felt her presence before I saw her face. I just wanted to help her so badly as she struggled with the material of her dress stuck in the door that eventually tore. Since that day and every time after that when I would see her, I would say, 'When A Man Finds A Wife.'"

"So you want to marry her?"

"Yes, I do!" Tony exclaims.

"I hope I live to see it," Genevieve's frail body is wracked with coughing. "Raise my bed up some more."

Concerned, Tony asks, "Should I call for a nurse?"

Mrs. Geneiveve says, "No need for that."

Mariah walks into the room and her face lights up as well as Tony's when they see each other. She really appreciates him being there for her mom but she stays focused and makes her way to her mom.

"How are you feeling today?" asks Mariah.

Brightly, Genevieve responds, "I feel like I'm going to make it. How about you?"

Making eye contact with Tony, Mariah says, "I'm feeling really blessed right now."

"Have you been by the nursing home to check on your father?" asks Genevieve.

"Yes Ma'am."

"Well......how is he?" Genevieve presses.

"The nurse says he has one more treatment."

Tony interjects, "What's wrong with your father? If you don't mind me asking."

Mariah says, "He's okay. He has colon cancer."

Standing up to leave, Tony says, "I'm sorry to hear that. Mrs. Genevieve it's always an honor to be in your company once again. I'll see you same time tomorrow."

Romantically, Tony pulls Mariah out of her chair. Embracing her with his arms around her back, he gently kisses her soft lips. Mariah is mesmorized by the sweet thought of his body touching hers. She's speechless when he pulls away.

Candance and Samuel walk in just as Tony leaves and make plans for Mariah after her graduation.

"I'll meet you here after your graduation to take you somewhere special," Tony says.

"Why here?" Mariah wonders.

"On behalf of your mother, I'm sure she would love to see you on your special night," Tony responds.

Candace chimes in, "Bye, Tony!"

As he leaves, Tony says, "See you guys later, and Mariah, I'll call you."

Turning back to Mariah, Candace wonders, "What are you waiting for, Mariah?"

Puzzled, Mariah asks, "What are you talking about?"

"You know, marriage!"

Mrs. Genevieve interrupts, "I know you're not talking. Don't you think you and Samuel should marry first?"

Surprised, Samuel says, "Oh! We're just friends."

Genevieve interrupts, "With benefits."

Mariah laughs, "Mom, they are really close friends. As a matter of fact, we all are."

Candace confirms, "Yeah, Mrs. Genevieve."

Genevieve says wryly, "So is everybody just going to tell me a lie on my bed of affliction? All right, time will tell."

Mariah is so excited to show her mother her degree that she has just earned. She walks into the hospital with her cap and gown on, with her degree in her hands along with flowers and a plaque to give to her mom for encouraging her through her college years. When she reaches the floor where her mom's room is, she notices nurses running in the direction of Mrs. Genevieve's room.

When she tries to leap over the physicians, Tony picks her up and carries her in his arms. Mariah is screaming and struggling to get away from Tony to reach her mother.

"You could've waited for me. I'm right here!" Mariah screams.

Tony takes Mariah to the hospital chapel and comforts her in his lap. He gently caresses her head and massages her with kisses on her head and hands.

Candace finds out that her best friend's mom has passed away when she finally reaches her room. She asked one of the nurses if they saw her daughter and one of them believed that she saw a young man going toward the chapel. When Candace finds her, she is laying in Tony's arms. She is relieved to know that someone was there when Mariah heard the news of her mother.

Candace stands at the door to pull herself together for her friend. Eventually, she works up her nerve to sit by her friend on the floor and hold her hands.

Chapter Nine

Mariah and her husband Tony are lying in bed on an early Friday morning. The alarm clock rings, and Mariah quickly reaches over to turn it off. She relaxes a bit before Monica comes bouncing in the room and jumps in bed with them. She snuggles up to her parents, looking sad and downhearted.

"Monica, what's wrong?" Mariah asks, holding her daughter's face in her hands.

"I don't want to go to school today."

"But it's just one more—"

"Awww, Mommy, please."

Tony wakes up. "What is she doing in here?"

"She wants to stay home with you today."

"What is today?" he asks.

"It's Friday!" Monica hollers.

"How do you know…"

"Because it's the day I want to stay home with you, Daddy. Please!" she begs.

"Oh, all right, all right! Why not?"

Monica jumps on top of him and wraps her arms around his neck. "Yay!"

Mariah gets up and enters the bathroom to get ready for work. "Hey, why don't you stay home with the rest of us?" Tony asks.

"If I do I will feel guilty. What if there's a child who needs me, and I'm not there to help them?" she answers, facing him.

"Well, in that case I consent. How about I fix you breakfast?"

"That sounds great!"

Mariah turns on her music and listens to her favorite song, "I Will Bless the Lord," while she puts her make-up on. Tony is in the kitchen fixing breakfast. Monica is eating her cereal at the breakfast table.

"What you cooking, Daddy?"

"Your mom's favorite." Tony puts the eggs on a plate, puts a piece of toast on the side and pours a glass of juice.

"Here comes Mommy."

"What's cooking, hon?" Mariah asks as she walks into the kitchen.

"Daddy made your favorites!" Monica says with a big smile.

"Eggs? You're my kind of guy!" Mariah says as she wraps her arms around him and kisses his cheek. "Do you mind if I get this to go?"

"Only if you promise to eat it!" Tony says smiling.

"Of course I will!"

The high school is filled with the noise of talking students, banging locker doors, morning announcements and bells ringing. Mariah is in her office. She has just finished her breakfast Tony made her. The secretary didn't see her come in.

Matthew, Samuel's brother, is a teacher there at the high school and has a problem that only Mrs. Mariah Chen can handle. "Is Mrs. Chen here yet?" he asks the secretary.

"No, I'm sorry. She usually doesn't come in until 8:30. Would you like to speak to the Assistant Principal?" she asks.

Mariah looks out her window and sees Matthew. She opens her door. "Matthew. What seems to be the problem?"

"Can I talk to you in your office?"

"Sure!" She motions him to come in. "Have a seat. What's going on?"

"There is a young man in my class who continues to harass a young lady about her shoes."

"What's wrong with her shoes?"

"Uh, they light up when she walks."

"Oh, ok. Well, send them in after the roll has been called."

"Yes, ma'am," Matthew says and walks out.

Mariah is going over her agenda for the day when there is a knock on her door. "You may enter," she says without looking up.

"There is a man here who wants to see you, ma'am," the secretary says, peeking her head in Mariah's office.

"Tell him to have a seat and I will be with him shortly."

"Certainly." The secretary shuts the door and walks to the man at the counter. "Please have a seat, sir. The principal will be with you shortly."

"Thank you," the man in overalls says as he takes a seat. He notices that all of the students in the school are wearing uniforms.

"When did they start wearing uniforms?" he asks the secretary.

"Ever since we got our new principal."

"So how long has he been here?"

"She," the secretary corrects him.

"She?" he asks.

"Yes, she has been here for about three years now. She came in and started changing everything. I've never seen anyone like her."

"What do you mean?"

"She has such a tender heart for children, and yet she is a very strong woman," the secretary says smiling. "I really admire her."

Just then the two students walk in from Mr. Matthew's class. "May I help you, young lady?" the secretary asks.

"We are supposed to talk to the principal."

"Well, have a seat. You'll have to wait a few minutes." The students take a seat and Mariah calls the secretary to tell her to send the man in. "The principal will see you now." The secretary points the way to the principal's office.

He walks to the door and knocks. "You may enter," Mariah says.

"Hello, Mrs…Mariah? Is that you?"

"Yes, in the flesh. Wait…Rodney. Why are you here?"

"I was coming for a job, but I guess I can forget about that now," Rodney says regretfully.

"Why would you say that?" Mariah asks.

"Look, I know the answer is no, so…"

"Why do you think that?"

"Because I know I did you a lot of wrong," he says, hanging his head.

"You didn't do anything wrong. You helped me to become the woman I am today. I don't blame anyone in my life. My life is not dictated by who helped or who hurt me. Opposition comes for two reasons: to trip us up or to give us stepping-stones to get us to where we need to be. I chose the stepping-stones. Now have a seat, Rodney, and quit jumping to conclusions." He sits down and begins to relax.

"So, tell me how I might be able to help you?" Mariah says as she sits down behind her desk.

"Well, first of all, I was looking for a job."

"What type?" she asks.

"Janitorial, but if you don't have anything, I understand."

"Do you have a diploma?"

"What kind of question is that?" he asks defensively.

"I have to ask that question of everyone. It also helps to know where to place you if nothing else is available."

"So, you are not trying to insult me?" he asks lowering his head.

"You think way too much, Rodney. I tell you what, go to the school board and tell them that I sent you for the maintenance job here. Then I will take it from there. Leave your number with my secretary, and I will call you sometime next week when I have more news," she says as she stands up.

"Thank you! Uh, what should I call you?"

"Mrs. Chen, at least here at the school."

"Then, thank you once again, Mrs. Mariah Chen!" he says with a smile.

"No problem. Have a nice day!" He walks out and the secretary brings the students in.

"Have a seat," she says as she is once again seated behind her desk. "What seems to be the problem here?"

"Raymond started making jokes about my shoes because they light up," the young lady said.

"But this is high school! Nobody wears Christmas lights on their tennis shoes," the young man says.

"You didn't have to make fun of me. Besides, I didn't know they lit up!"

"What do you mean you didn't know?"

"You heard me!" the young lady snaps back at him. They both begin arguing back and forth.

"Wait just a minute!" Mariah hollers. "We will not have this in here. Now you listen. You're not here for the Christmas or for the lights." Raymond laughs.

"Raymond," she says sternly. "She cannot help what her parents can or cannot afford. Be careful, young man! The same can happen to you and your family... or worse!" Mariah softens the tone of her voice. "Young lady, don't let this bring you down. Keep your head held high. You never know what good can come out of this if you keep a good attitude about things that are uncomfortable." She turns her attention to Raymond. "This is a warning to you! Both of you go back to class. Let it be known that if anyone else says anything to you about this I will SUSPEND them. Is that understood?" They both nod their heads.

"Thank you, Mrs. Chen. You're the best!" the young lady says on her way out the door. Mariah just smiles at her. On the way back to class Raymond apologizes.

"I'm sorry for teasing you. It won't happen again."

"I know it won't," she says with a smile.

Chapter Ten

Candace is getting out of her car in front of the courthouse to go over some paperwork with her colleague. Janice has been waiting in her car for Candace to arrive. When she sees her, she gets out and runs to Candace. "Candace, may I have a word with you?"

"Excuse me, but do I know you?" Candace asks, searching her face for some recognition.

"Yes, it's Janice!"

"Janice from middle school?"

"Yes, I…"

"What's wrong with you?" Candace interrupts. "You look different!"

"I need you to talk to Mariah for me!"

"Now, why on earth would I do that?"

"Please, Candace! It is VERY important!" Janice says, begging.

"You know Mariah has nothing to say to you, and I, for one, don't blame her!"

"I know what I did was wrong, but I desperately need to talk to her."

"Janice. I do not want you anywhere near my friend!"

"Could you please just tell her to contact me in her spare time?" she says pleading.

"What did I just say?" Candace begins to walk away. Janice runs after her and makes Candace look her in the face. "Candace, give me a chance! I know I did wrong, but please, I BEG you!" Janice says with tears in her eyes.

"Fine! Give me your number. I will contact her. You, on the other hand, don't ever show up at my job again. What's the number?"

"555-2034. Thanks, Candace!"

"Whatever!" Candace writes the number down and walks off. Janice stands just watching her leave. Finally, she walks slowly back to her car. She gets in the seat, closes the door and puts her head in her hands to cry.

Jasmine calls Mariah's home phone. No one is there so she leaves a message. "Hey, Mariah! It's been a while. I want to know if I might be able to stay at your house for a couple of days. I can't wait to see my cousin! I'll be there tomorrow evening sometime. Bye!"

Tony and Monica are at McDonald's. Monica is eating a Happy Meal and Tony ordered a large fry and a drink. Janice walks in and orders a burger and a parfait.

"Daddy, can we call Mommy?" Monica asks.

"Mommy is at work, baby."

"I know, but I just want to hear her voice."

"Yeah, me too. All right, I'll call, but if she takes too long to answer then that's it. No more phone calls."

"Ok, deal!" Monica says with a big smile.

He dials the number and the phone begins to ring. After just two rings, Mariah picks up.

"Hello?"

"Hey, baby!" Tony says, winking at Monica.

"Hey, sweetie! What are you two up to?"

"We are at Monica's favorite place."

"McDonald's again?" she says laughing.

"Yep!"

"Well, tell her I said hi." Tony gives Monica the phone.

"Hi, Mommy! Come join us."

"Hi, sweetie! Sorry, but Mommy can't. Give your daddy the phone now."

Janice sits down beside them as Monica hands her dad the phone.

"Hello? Tony? Tony, are you there? Hello?"

"Mariah? Mariah, you're breaking up. Hello, Mariah?" At the sound of Mariah's name, Janice turns her head and focuses her attention on them.

"What's wrong, Daddy?" Monica asks.

"Your mom's phone is giving her problems."

Janice is really curious to know if they are related to the Mariah she knows and needs to talk to. "Excuse me. Are you Mariah's husband?" Janice asks.

"Monica, wrap it up, baby," Tony says to Monica before he turns to answer.

"Uh, that would depend on the last name," Tony asks, wondering who she is.

"Mariah Davis."

"Well, she is a Chen now. I am her husband, and you are?

"Oh, I'm sorry. My name is Janice. Mariah and I were friends in middle school."

"Is that so?"

"It is. I have been trying to reach her. How is she?"

"She's great. She is the principal at the high school."

"That's awesome. I always knew she would succeed."

"Daddy, I'm ready now," Monica says with ketchup on her face.

"Oh, and this must be your daughter."

"Yes, this is our little princess," he says with a proud grin as he wipes the ketchup off Monica's face.

"Hello, Monica. My name is Janice." Monica smiles and waves.

"Well, ma'am, I'm sorry, but we really need to go. I will tell Mariah that I saw you."

"Nice meeting you!" she said and waved to Monica as they walked out the door. Janice leaves right behind them. She was desperate to talk to Mariah. One way or another she would get her chance.

"I'm leaving early," Mariah says to the secretary. "Please tell my assistant to put any papers I need to address on my desk. See you Monday!"

"Have a good weekend!" the secretary replies with a smile.

"You too!" Mariah answers as she walks out the door.

She gets in her car and heads for home. Janice has been parked at the school waiting for her. She follows her home. Mariah pulls up in front of her house and sees that Tony's car is there. Janice parks the car and jumps out to catch Mariah before she goes in.

"I need your help!" Janice hollers at Mariah.

"Help for what? Do I know you?"

"Mariah, I'm your girl, Janice!"

"Janice, what?" Mariah looks at her with a strange expression. "Why are you here, and how do you know where I live? Have you been stalking me?"

At that moment, Tony comes out of the house.

"Baby, what's going on?" he asks Mariah.

"I just need to talk to you," Janice explains.

"Hey, you're that lady from McDonald's," Tony says.

"I need to go check on my child!" Mariah says and turns to walk into the house.

"But Mariah, please!" Janice begs and falls to her knees.

Mariah ignores her and enters the house, leaving Tony outside with Janice.

"Apparently, she does not want to talk to you. Please leave and don't come back until my wife invites you here!" He turns and goes into the house and closes the door.

Chapter Eleven

Janice gets in her car to leave. She leans over the steering wheel and begins to cry. She then starts her car and drives to the park where she and Mariah spent time together in middle school, the place they would talk as friends before the summer when she destroyed their friendship.

Janice goes to the veranda and sits on the picnic table where she and Mariah spent hours talking. She suddenly remembers what led her to lose her best friend. She relives it as if it were yesterday.

"Janice, what's wrong?" Mariah asks Janice, seeing the look on her face.

"Nothing," Janice snaps and rudely walks away. Jasmine sees what just took place and follows Janice to her class.

"Hey, Janice, do you want to hang out tonight?"

"Why do you want to hang out with me?" she asks.

"To be honest, I really think Christopher deserves you instead of Mariah. She's not good enough for him."

"Do you really think so?"

"Yes, I really do!" Jasmine says, baiting her.

"But she's my friend," Janice says hanging her head.

"Girl, you need to be your own friend. Besides, do you like him? Of course you do. I've seen the way you look at him. Listen, Chris is sick. You should go over there after school."

"But what about his mom?" Janice asks.

"She is never home! She is always away on business trips."

"So, what am I supposed to do?"

"Cheer him up!"

"How am I supposed to do that?"

"Oh, Girl, I'm sure you'll think of something when you see him," Jasmine says with a devilish grin and a wink.

Christopher is lying in bed. His brother is getting ready to go out with his friends when there is a knock on the door. His brother opens the door to see Janice standing outside in a real sexy outfit. "Hi, is Chris here?"

"He's in his room."

"I heard he wasn't feeling well and wanted to make sure he was ok. Can I go see him?" Janice asks shyly.

"Sure." He hollers at Chris, "Hey, I'm outta here! Later!"

Janice walks back to Chris' room. "What are you doing here?" Chris asks, staring her up and down.

"I thought you could use some company since I heard you were sick and not able to come to school."

"Well, that was very thoughtful of you," he replies still staring at her. "Are you going somewhere after you leave here?"

"Why do you ask?" she replies, kind of puzzled.

"Well, because you look…so hot! You know in a good way," he says.

"Thank you, but this is how I dress after school."

"I think you better get out of here before I do something to you," Chris says, starting to advance toward her.

"You can't. You're sick, remember?" she says teasingly.

"Hey, I may be sick, but I'm not dead!" Christopher gets out of bed and walks into his bathroom to wash his face. He's only in his boxers. Janice sits down on his bed. He comes back in and sits down beside her. "Can I touch you?" he asks longingly.

"If it makes you feel better," she answers. She closes her eyes and feels chills rush over her body at his touch. She feels his lips on her neck and desires him more and more. Their lips begin to collaborate. Desire intensifies in both of them.

Kevin comes home to find Mariah knocking on the door. "What are you doing here?" he asks.

"I came to check on Christopher," she replies. "Can I go see him?"

"Sure," he says, opening the door. "He's in his room."

Mariah walks in and walks toward Chris' room. She pushes open the door and finds Christopher and Janice making out. "How could you!" she hollers and turns to run out.

"Mariah!" Christopher and Janice both holler.

Janice is suddenly snapped back to the present. She hangs her head and cries even harder. She regrets the mistakes she's made and the friendship she destroyed. She pulls herself together and leaves the park.

Mariah and Tony are sitting in their living room. Mariah is feeling a little down about the day's events. The phone rings and Tony gets up to answer it. "Hello?"

"Hi, Tony, it's Candace. Is Mariah there?"

"Sure, hold on a moment," he says, handing the phone to Mariah. "It's Candace."

"Hello, Candace."

"How are you doing?" Candace asks.

"I'm ok, what's going on?"

"You'll never believe who's trying to reach you!"

"Janice," she says matter-of-factly.

"How did you know?" Candace asks, surprised.

"She showed up in front of our house. I think she is stalking me. Tony told her to leave our property. I have nothing to say to her."

"Mariah, you can't be like that. It must be important for her to suddenly try reach out to you. Listen, I'm not fond of her either and what she did was definitely wrong. The whole stalking thing, well, that's just plain crazy. However, I think you need to hear her out. Maybe this is what both of you need to so you can move on. Why don't we meet at the library?"

"Uh, no. That's not good," Mariah says.

"Ok, where then? The park?" Candace asks.

"Um, that might work."

"Ok. I will call Janice now and tell her."

"Good night, Candace," Mariah says.

"I'll talk to you tomorrow," Candace replies and they hang up the phone.

Mariah takes a deep breath and lets out a deep sigh. Tony takes a long look at her. "Come on, baby. Let's go to bed."

"Where's Monica?"

"She's asleep already," he says, standing up. He reaches down and takes Mariah's hand and pulls her up. He wraps his arm around her waist and walks her back to the bedroom.

Janice is already at the park, waiting. Mariah gets out of the car and heads to their old spot in the veranda. Candace pulls up with Samuel and then walks alongside Mariah to the park. As the two of them walk up to Janice, Mariah prays under her breath. *Lord, please don't let me act like a fool. Help me to exercise patience and love.*

"Thank you for having a change of heart," Janice says earnestly.

Mariah and Candace sit down at the picnic table. "What's going on?" Mariah asks.

"You look great, and you have such a beautiful family. What do you do at the school?"

"I am the principal," Mariah replies.

"My God! That's great! An awesome career too. Has much changed?"

"Yes, everyone wears uniforms now."

"That is a big change!"

"I guess I had to go through the hurt I endured so something good could come of it."

"That's true," Candace says looking intently at Mariah. "You really have a good heart. Most people are only concerned about themselves and never help anyone."

"Ok, enough about that. What was so important that you needed to talk to me about that made you act like a crazy woman?"

"First, I want to tell you how sorry I am for what Chris and I did," Janice says, lowering her head in shame.

"Why, on earth did you do it?"

"First, because I was jealous that you had all of the attention of all the popular guys and you didn't even dress as nice as I did. Second," she paused a moment, "Jasmine helped me."

"What? What do you mean?" Janice explains to Mariah how Jasmine set her up to go to Christopher's house that day after school when he was sick and make out with him. She also told her the things that Jasmine said about her.

"Are you serious?" Mariah asks.

"Yes."

"But still. How could you when you knew how Jasmine was treating me at home and the things she was saying to me? You were supposed to be my friend, Janice."

"I know. I am so sorry, Mariah. I was caught up in the moment," Janice says remorsefully.

"You know, I am all right, though. I am happily married now and have a beautiful daughter and a great career. That was the past and it will stay there. So, is that it? Is that all you have to tell me?"

"No," Janice says, looking away as tears start to fill her eyes. "I am sick."

"What is it? You have a cold?"

"I wish it was only a cold," she says, fighting back tears. "I tested positive for AIDS. I have AIDS, Mariah."

"What? Oh, Janice, no. I am so sorry," Mariah says, shaking her head. "When did you find out?"

"A couple of days ago," she whispers as she wipes her eyes.

"Are you being treated?"

"No, I don't want to get treated. If people find out I have AIDS they won't want to be around me. I can't handle rejection, Mariah."

"But you are rejecting a longer life by rejecting treatment, Janice."

Samuel gets out of the car and walks up to them. "So, is everything cool?" he asks Mariah and Candace.

"Yes, it's fine."

"So, you brought a bodyguard, did ya?" Janice asks.

"No, more like a support system."

"Listen, if you want to hang with us, feel free," Candace says to Janice.

"Thank you! That is very considerate of you, but I think I will pass." Janice stands up and gives Mariah a hug and says goodbye. She walks away to her car. Mariah, Candace and Samuel return to their vehicles.

"So, how do you feel?" Samuel asks Mariah.

"I'm not sure," she says. "I have clarity about the past, but now the future is bothering me."

"I'm not sure I understand what you mean," Samuel says with a puzzled look on his face.

"The reason Janice was seeking out Mariah is because she is very sick."

"Is it cancer?" Samuel asks.

"If it was, I could accept that, but no. It is something that can affect a lot of people. The people she has intercourse with."

"Oh, my Lord. Janice has Herpes!" Samuel exclaims.

"No. Janice has AIDS," Mariah explains. "And it hurts because I told her when we used to come here as kids that she needed to be careful before she got a disease."

"You shouldn't feel bad," Candace says. "You tried to warn her. It was her own wrongdoing. You know that warning comes before destruction. You did your part in warning her, Mariah."

"I told her to go get treated and to stop rejecting herself."

"Let's pray that she listens this time," Samuel suggests.

"God knows how to get through to everyone, huh, Samuel," Mariah says, turning to him.

"Yeah, I guess."

"You guess?" Candace says. "Did you stop eating those Little Debbie cakes?"

"Oh, yeah, you're right!" he says.

"Samuel, I never realized that Matthew was your brother," Mariah suddenly turns to look at him.

"Actually, he still is!" Matthew says teasingly.

"You know what I mean," she says, punching him playfully.

"Everyone was ashamed of me," he says. "Even I was ashamed of myself, but people can change. I, for one, am very happy!"

"Wait a minute!" Mariah exclaims. "The two of you came here together?"

"Well, uh, I…" Candace stutters.

"Well, I NOTHING! You two are hiding something from me!" she says with a grin.

"But we were…" Candace starts to explain.

"You know what? I already knew!" she says throwing up her hand at them. She gets in her car and rolls down the window. "I better be in the wedding!"

Samuel and Candace laugh and get into Samuel's car.

Chapter Twelve

Jasmine has been at Mariah's house with Tony and Monica for about thirty minutes. Tony is anxiously awaiting Mariah's return from her meeting with Janice. Jasmine has lost twenty pounds, has extremely short hair and is wearing a long, tight dress. She is totally broke. Tony feels very uncomfortable sitting in the living room with Jasmine.

"Mariah always knew how to pick 'em," she says, winking at Tony.

"Jasmine…"

"You can call me Jazzy," she says flirtatiously.

"I'm sorry, but there is nothing jazzy about you. I prefer to call you Jasmine. Besides, even if I wasn't with Mariah, I still wouldn't give you the time of day. Mariah is the best thing that ever happened to me. She has always been beautiful inside and out."

"Mariah ain't nothing!" she says angrily. "I bet she was still a virgin when you met her."

"Is THAT supposed to be a bad thing?" he asks.

"Well, I guess not if you are OLD FASHIONED!" she says sarcastically.

"Mariah should be here any minute. Hopefully, she will kick you out!"

Mariah walks through the kitchen door and lays her purse on the table. "Honey, I'm back!" She walks into the living room. "What on earth are YOU doing here?" she asks, looking at Jasmine in shock.

"Didn't you get my message?" she asks.

"What message?"

"The one I sent you yesterday saying that I was coming today."

"Girl, please! Had I known you were coming I would have gone on vacation!"

"Mariah, that was cold!" Jasmine snaps.

"No! COLD is you helping my best friend to sleep with the guy who liked ME!"

"I didn't MAKE her do anything! That girl had a mind of her own," Jasmine says flippantly.

"Tell me why you are here."

"Because I miss my family."

"What FAMILY?" Mariah asks sarcastically. "Not THIS one! We were never close. We didn't even LIKE each other. So, how long are you planning on staying?"

"Well, all I need is…"

"Three days!" Mariah interrupts.

"Three days? I need more time than that!"

"I have spoken and that is final! You have three days and you are out of here!"

"But you didn't consult with your husband!" she says snidely.

"I don't need to and stop being concerned about what's MINE!"

Jasmine flashes her a dirty look as Mariah walks towards the spare bedroom. "This is where you will sleep. Most importantly, here are the rules. No lingerie. You are to have clothes on under your robe. Nothing transparent! Nothing revealing! When I have to leave and my husband is here by himself, YOU LEAVE!"

"Where am I supposed to go?"

"That sounds like a personal problem!"

"Oh, I see. You are scared that I will take your man," Jasmine says sarcastically.

"Jasmine, please! Don't flatter yourself! You just have a past that I do not want ruining our reputations."

"Mariah, people can change."

"Yes, they can, but YOU haven't!"

"How do you know that?"

"Because of your choice of words, actions and even your dress!" she says and turns to walk away. "I am tired and I am going to bed. We will talk tomorrow. Good night!"

"HMMMM!" Jasmine says and stomps over to the bed.

Mariah goes in and checks on Monica. She is sleeping. Tony is lying in bed, reading and waiting on his wife. Mariah goes in to take a shower and then joins her husband. "Are you all right, sweetie?" he asks.

"Yes, I'm fine," she says with a deep sigh.

"So, tell me, do you think she will make it here for three days?" Tony asks with a wink.

"I have no idea!"

"So, how did things go with Janice?"

"Not good. Not good at all, baby."

"So, tell me about it," he says taking her in his arms as she climbs into bed.

"She has AIDS."

"Are you serious?" he asks tenderly. Tony turns her face toward his. "How do you feel?"

"How do you think I feel? I warned her about that years ago and now it has come to pass. I don't know if I should tell Jasmine or not."

"Why would you do that?" he asks.

"It's a long story and right now, I just want to get some rest."

"Whatever you feel in your heart you should do. Maybe it will help her look at life a little differently."

"Maybe you're right," she says before kissing him. She lays her head on the pillow and closes her eyes. Deep down inside, her heart is breaking, and she is fighting back the tears.

Over an hour later, Mariah still cannot fall asleep. There is way too much on her heart and mind. She gets up quietly and goes to the kitchen. Jasmine is up and sitting at the table.

"What's up with you?" she asks sarcastically. "You worried I might be checking on your husband?"

"Jasmine, you say one more thing about my husband and you will see more stars than Hollywood!"

"You still passing out threats?"

"Not threats. Promises!" she says angrily. "And one more thing…why did you make Janice sleep with Christopher?" she was now yelling.

"What are you talking about? Who's—" Jasmine pauses, remembering who Mariah was talking about. "Oh yeah. Those two. Why are you trying to bring up the past? Are you happily married, or do you still have feelings for somebody else?" Jasmine asks, taunting her.

"Janice has AIDS!" Mariah blurts out at her.

"What?" Jasmine falls to the floor and begins to cry.

"Why you crying so much?" Mariah asks, turning her face from Jasmine.

"When did she find out? Is she getting treatment?" Jasmine asks through her tears.

"A couple of days ago, and after the talk I had with her earlier, I hope so. You still have not answered my question, Jasmine!"

"Janice slept with Kevin to get back at me for hurting you," Jasmine says through tears.

"So, why would you say that to me now?"

"I haven't been totally honest with you."

"Gee, that is not surprising!" Mariah says.

"I didn't just come here to see you, but I..."

"Just get to the point. Will you, Jasmine? I'm tired of your games."

"I'm not playing any games. Not this time. Can we please go sit on the couch?"

"I'm not sure what you are going to say, but just say it!"

"I came back here to see how I got this disease, Mariah."

"I hope you are talking about hypertension and not some..."

"I have the same thing as Janice!"

"No, Jazzy, Janice has AIDS! You can't mean the same thing she has!"

"Yes, I slept with so many guys, I had no idea who I got it from, but then when you said that Janice had it... well, it just makes sense now."

"What do you mean?"

"I mean, Kevin. I now know he was born with HIV. Janice slept with him and now she has AIDS. Someone had told me that Kevin was born with HIV but I didn't believe it because I thought he loved me enough to mention that. I slept with him and I have it."

Mariah falls to the kitchen floor now too and joins Jasmine. She has tears in her eyes. "Jasmine, when were you going to tell me? What if you would have come on to my husband and in a moment of weakness he would have…"

"No, Mariah, I promise! I wasn't going to try anything. I really promise! I just had to come here to be with someone who loves me. I can't handle anymore rejection, Mariah!" She buries her head in her hands and breaks down into sobs. "Please, help me!"

"I don't know how to help you. I'm not God! I can't fix this. Your sins have caught up with you."

"I know, Mariah. Don't you think I know that? I just need someone to show me a little compassion. That is why I came to YOU!" She starts crying uncontrollably.

Mariah moves closer and rubs her back. "I'm sorry, Jazzy. I am so sorry!"

At that moment, Tony walks in the kitchen to see why the two girls were yelling. He gets on the floor next to his wife and holds her as she tries to console Jasmine.

Chapter Thirteen

Candace and Samuel are planning their wedding several days later. "How much do you love me?" she suddenly asks him.

"Why, you're the best thing that ever happened to me. You are my world. If you were not in it I would cease to exist," he replies.

"Oh, Samuel! That is so sweet of you to say!"

"Well, I mean it!" He reaches over and takes her face in his hands and kisses her. The telephone rings as they kiss. Candace starts to pull away to answer the phone. "Oh, don't answer it," Samuel says, enjoying the moment.

"I don't want to, but I need to," she replies regretfully.

"Oh, all right. Go ahead."

"Hello?" she says, picking up the receiver.

"Hello, may I speak to Candace please?" the nurse on the other end says.

"Speaking."

"My name is Cynthia from the Medical Center. Janice Marssino wanted me to call and let her friends know that she is getting treated for her condition."

"Thank you!" Candace says elatedly. "That is great news. Tell her congratulations and I will let the others know."

"Would you like to write down the information and address where we are located? I'm sure she would love a phone call or a visit."

"Sure! What is it?" The nurse gives Candace the information and she writes it down. "Ok, thank you!" she says and they hang up.

"Who was that and what was that all about?" Samuel asks.

"That was a nurse down at the Medical Center. Janice decided to get treated."

"Oh, that is terrific news!"

"Yes, it is and I cannot wait to tell Mariah."

Mariah takes Jasmine down to the same Medical Center where Janice is being treated. The doctors and nurses begin assisting Jasmine. Mariah takes a seat in the waiting room and waits for Jasmine to get situated in her room. She picks up a magazine and begins reading. Soon her phone rings. It is her father who is in the hospital. She tells the nurses at the nurses' station that she has an emergency and rushes out.

Mariah makes it to the hospital where her father is and inquires as to where he is. The nurse leads Mariah to the ICU. She knocks and enters the room the nurse said he's in.

"Daddy!" she exclaims.

"Aww, look. It's my baby," he whispers and then coughs.

"How are you doing, Daddy? I came as fast as I could."

"I've been waiting for you," he says and coughs again. "Mariah, I've neglected you your whole life. You could have easily done the same to me, but I know that just isn't you. You would never treat me that way. There are few people on this earth like you, baby. Please stay that way. Don't ever let anybody or anything change you." He coughs again. "By the way, thank you for paying my medical bill. Now…I know it is…my time to go," he says and gets choked up. "But, I wanted your face to be the last face I see before I leave this world." His eyes fill up with tears.

"Daddy, no! I have plans for us!" Mariah cries and goes to her father's side.

"Mariah save your plans for someone else who needs what you have to give. I have cursed you and you have only blessed me. Don't ever stop blessing people.

This world is cruel and can be so cold. This world needs people like you. Go now, my precious little girl! I need to go now so that your face is the last I see. Go on now." He smiles at her and closes his eyes.

Mariah squeezes his hand and whispers, "I love you, Daddy." She lets go and heads for the door. The machines start ringing, but she never looks back. "Code Blue in ICU! Code Blue in ICU!" blares over the loud speaker as she walks out the door with tears streaming down her face.

Mariah stays busy in the organization she incorporated for young boys and girls in the community. Twice a month each child completes a challenge that helps them to explore their strength. Every three months she exposes them to a place they have never been. At the beginning of the year, she hosts a graduation for those who are moving to the next level. There are 5 levels to obtain.

Her motto is: Believe In Me And I will Grow, Believe In You And I Will Never Know. That means, If I believe that I can do what you did then I'm growing, but if I believe that only you can do it and I never try, then I will never know. Mariah also has a cabin called the Celibacy Club. Every weekend a parent volunteers to encourage teenagers to keep themselves for marriage. There are so many fun exercises and activities to do that other schools join them for a conference where there is guest speaker.

Mariah has helped so many people who asked for her assistance, including her cousin Jasmine. She talked to the School Board about allowing Jasmine to bring awareness to the students about celibacy and she encourages them to join the Celibacy Club. Jasmine is paid enough money at her new job to allow her to move into her own place. She is thrilled with her brand new life. Janice, on the other hand, moves to another state.

When Mariah finally decides to visit her, it is too late. She begins to feel guilty but the fact that she forgave her means much more than her being able to say good bye.

Six months later, Mariah and her family are on their way to Candace and Samuel's wedding. As Tony is driving to the church, she ponders on how so many of the obstacles have been overcome in her life, her family and her friends.

Mariah is standing at the altar with her best friend. She smiles at her and winks at Candace who is a beautiful bride. Samuel beams at her from ear to ear.

"I now pronounce you, Husband and Wife!" The pastor says. "You may kiss your bride!"

Books the Author Read During Her Journey for *Insurmountable* (Recommended Reading)

1. The Bible

2. *The Comfort Trap or What If You're Riding A Dead Horse* by Judith Sills, Ph.D.

3. *Commanding your Morning* by Dr. Cindy Trimm

4. *Favor, The Road to Success: How to Receive Special Favor with God and People* by Bob Buess

5. *Prayers that Rout Demons* by John Eckhardt

Church Acknowledgements

- Kingdom of God Church in Jeanerette, Louisiana

- New Beginning Word of Faith Ministries in Four Corners, Louisiana

- St. Moses Baptist Church in Sorrel , Louisiana

Songs that encouraged the author

- "The Denied Stone" by Vanessa Bell Armstrong

- "Worshipper" by Canton Jones

- "Run Wild" by For King & Country (featuring Andy Mineo)

- "Something Inside So Strong" by Vanessa Bell Armstrong

- "Broken" by Shekinah Glory

- "Walking Shoes" by Mali

- "Things I Can't Change" by Willie Banks

- "My World Needs You" by Kirk Franklin (featuring Sarah Reeves, Tasha Cobbs & Tamela Mann)

- "Couldn't Tell It" by Karen Clark Sheard

- "Soon I Will Be Done" by Naturally 7 (featuring Mahalia)

- "Nobody Cared" by Canton Jones

(Just to name a few)

About the Author

Anna Colar, a native of Jeanerette, Louisiana, lives a wholesome life. She teaches theatre, vocals and character building in her local area. She studied Performing Arts and is a Film major. Anna is an aspiring film maker and *Insurmountable* is her first novel. She has a son named Isaiah whom she loves and is proud to be his mom.